The Other Side of the Moon

By Prisha Shivani

J. Mark Price Reading, LLC Publications

The Other Side of the Moon

By Prisha Shivani

Cover design: concept by Prisha Shivani, Illustrator Tatiana Minina

Editors: Mark Price and Lindsey Bainbridge

J. Mark Price Reading, LLC Publications

Dedications

To Mom and Dad, who have encouraged me ever since
I started writing.

To Mr. Mark Price, for taking his time every week to
edit the book with me.

This book would not exist without all of your help.
Thank you.

Daniel

Daniel was very excited. He had been waiting for his trip to the moon, and now he was finally going. He looked out the window of the spaceship. Everything was getting smaller and smaller and smaller. The houses looked like toy homes while the cars looked like tiny, colorful ants. The trees seemed like mere branches and twigs. As the spaceship ascended higher and higher, the sky turned from aqua to indigo to pitch-dark black.

"Daniel, we are almost at the moon," Lily, one of the pilots, called.

"Eat something before you step out on the moon, Daniel," Buzz suggested. Buzz, the co-pilot, was flying his fifth mission to the moon, so he was slightly less nervous than Lily, who was flying her first.

Daniel walked into the MCR (Mission Control Room), ate some crackers, and looked around. It was filled with red buttons and metallic levers.

"When I step out, you guys can take a break, but please be on the lookout," Daniel said, chewing the last cracker. "I'm about to put on my space suit, and then I will climb down from the ship and onto the moon's surface. I should be back in no more than 45 minutes."

"Sure," Buzz replied. "But Daniel, remember ... *strange things happen on the moon.*" Buzz's words echoed around the ship, making them sound even more mysterious. Daniel flashed Buzz a curious look, pulled on his space suit, and exited the spaceship. As the door closed, Daniel waved goodbye to Lily and Buzz.

Standing on the moon, Daniel looked down at the dull, white surface. To his great surprise, he noticed a red space rock. And not just one red space rock, but a whole trail of them!

Suspicious, Daniel thought. *Why would there be red rocks if the moon is white?* He started following the rocks and collecting them as he went. After he had walked for what felt like a mile, the trail stopped, and he realized he was lost. He looked into the distance, across the moon, and all he saw was complete darkness. *Buzz was right*, Daniel thought, *strange things are happening on the moon.* "Now I am just lost," Daniel muttered aloud.

"I think I can help you with that," piped up an unfamiliar voice.

Daniel turned slowly around to see a creature that was white with gray stripes. One of its eyes was pink and the other blue.

Daniel was able to find his voice and uttered a few words, "W-W-Who are you?"

"I'm the Queen's messenger; I'm called a Sqoonafant. I am on a mission to find an alien from the 'Otherworld.'" The Sqoonafant's voice was very high-pitched, like a squeaky clarinet.

"Are there more of you?" Daniel asked.

"No. And I did not always look like this. I was cursed to look this way." The Sqoonafant looked like it was about to cry.

Daniel quickly changed the subject. "So, about the messenger thing, why do you need to find an 'alien?'"

The Sqoonafant sniffed and replied, "The kingdom does not know many details, but here is the rumor:

"The dark side of the moon has a portal, and to get into our world you have to transport through that portal. If you just climb in, you would be in complete darkness. When you move through the portal you arrive in our city. In the center of the city there is a heart-shaped jewel that is cut in half. This jewel makes our city the way it is, so if there is no jewel, no city! But recently our city has been fading even

though the jewel is still there. It's a
mystery.

"The Council is still determining what happened, but I already *know* what happened, because I saw it myself. And that is why I was cursed to become this creature I am now. I am the messenger, so I'm only supposed to deliver the message, not tell the whole story, but I will tell you anyway.

"It was the witches! I saw the witches steal the jewel and replace it. That is why I need an alien; it was the Queen's orders. She thinks that aliens are strong and brave and might be able to get the jewel back from the witches."

"Wow, that was quite a story," Daniel breathed, "and I have decided that I will help you, even though I am not an alien."

"Thank you!" exclaimed the Sqoonafant. "By the way, my name is Pinky."

"Okayyyyy, Pinky! Where is the portal?" Daniel said.

"Right here," said Pinky, as he gestured toward a large dark spot hovering in the air. Daniel's eyes grew wide as he took in the portal: it looked like large bands of indigo color swirling around in waves, creating an opening at its center.

"Before we go into the portal, Pinky, what were the red rocks for that I saw?"

Pinky grew very quiet. "Those were witches' footprints."

"Wow! That was not the answer I thought it would be, but, okay."

And so they walked into the portal!

Lily and Buzz

"WHERE IS DANIEL?" Lily roared. "I've lost connection on the walkie-talkie."

She was holding her space suit in her right hand and walkie-talkie in her left. The windows were icing over. *It must be cold out there*, she thought. But it was toasty warm inside the ship.

"How long has he been gone?" asked Buzz.

"At least an hour," Lily replied.

"How about we go find him?" suggested Buzz.

They pulled on their suits and stepped out of the ship. And when they stepped out ... they saw the same red rocks that Daniel had seen.

"Let's collect them, and follow the trail," Lily exclaimed.

And so they were traveling on the same path as Daniel.

Or were they?

Finally, they saw the end of the path.

"Where are we?" asked Buzz.

"Don't know, but isn't it weird that there is that indigo swirl in the darkness?"

"Oh yeah!" Buzz exclaimed, looking carefully at it.

Lily moved toward the swirl and slowly reached her index finger closer to the strange sight. Her fingertip grazed the middle of the midnight-blue spinning circle.

"What is the password?" said an unfamiliar voice.

"Eeehhh!" screamed Lily as she jumped back.

"Cor*rect*! The password is *one jump back*."

The indigo swirl split in half like a karate master had just kicked it.

"I don't think we should go in there," Buzz said, his voice shaking.

But it was too late; Lily had jumped inside the portal.

"Does she ever listen to me? Nope, she just does whatever she wants to,"

Buzz grumbled as he walked inside the portal.

"Buzz, where are you?" Lily cried.

"Here!"

"Turn on your flashlight!"

"Okay, that's much better," Buzz declared, as he looked around and saw two pathways carved into the stone wall in front of them.

They looked exactly alike, two black holes moving into the darkness in separate directions.

"I'll go through that path," she said, pointing to the opening on the right, and you go through the other one," Lily said.

Buzz moved into the tunnel on the left, as Lily had assigned him. Everywhere he shined his flashlight made circles of illumination, small moons in the darkness.

"Lily, are you there?" Buzz said into his walkie-talkie.

"Yes!" Lily replied.

"Do you see anything?"

"Well, there is another black circle – this one is spinning too, even faster than the first."

"I think I've hit a dead end in my tunnel," Buzz said into his walkie-talkie. "I'll come over to your side."

They were standing in front of the portal together. "What do you reckon I should do when I touch the portal this time?" Lily asked.

"How about *two* jumps this time?"

"Okay."

Lily touched the portal and jumped two jumps back.

"*Innn*correct," said the same strange voice.

Suddenly the ground rumbled as if it was hungry. Some of the ground around them broke off and was replaced with steaming hot lava.

"Hey, look at that button," Lily exclaimed, pointing to the ground directly between them. The button embedded in the ground was a dark grass green, with a black stripe running through its middle.

"I'm going to press it!" yelled Buzz excitedly.

"No, we don't know what it does!" Lily exclaimed.

"Well, then what will we do?" Buzz asked as he started walking toward Lily.

"We could –" Lily started.

"OWWW!"

Buzz was on the floor and it looked as if he had tripped. The problem was that he was on the button.

"Correct! The password is *falling on the button*," announced the monitor in its robotic voice.

The portal opened, and they climbed through.

Daniel

Daniel looked around, astonished, his mouth hanging open. There was Twizzlers candy, shaped into what looked like a tree with reddish-black branches that ended in claws. There were animals in fading colors, half pink, half gray or black.

"Where are we going?" Daniel asked.

"To the Queen's castle!" replied Pinky. "She wants to see the alien."

"Where is the castle?"

"Look up."

The castle was beautiful. It was silver all over and very sparkly. They hiked the rest of the way, through the castle doors, and into its main hall.

"Um, why is no one here?"

Pinky looked speechless. "Maridia!" Pinky exclaimed. "What happened?"

"I-It was the witches. They just barged in with the trolls and monsters and took everyone with them ... even the Queen!" Maridia said, looking around wildly. Her eyes came to rest on Daniel. "Who are you?" she asked, pointing to him.

"My name is Daniel. Just asking, but if they took everyone, why are you here?"

"I hid behind one of those," she pointed, indicating several thick, white, marble columns. "And I guess they didn't see me."

"What should we do?" asked Pinky.

"Let's go to where the witches are ... isn't it called the Witches' Lair?"

"Good idea!" Maridia said.

Lily, Buzz and ... Daniel?

"Ow, that hurts! You stepped on my foot, Buzz! It is so tight walking through here."

"Well, now you say it. You are the one that wanted to go through the portal, Lily."

They had gone through the portal carefully but had been seen by moss-green creatures dressed in black. The creatures' skin was dry and leathery, and their midnight-colored eyes were as big as the bottoms of soda bottles. Seeing the creatures, Buzz and Lily turned back toward the portal, meaning to run back through. But the portal had vanished! The creatures chased them toward a large, iron door. Throwing open the door and charging through, they saw a narrow pathway leading straight through the center of the room. Along either side of the path were rusty, old steel cages with bolted doors holding prisoners. The prisoners were sitting on the floors of their cages, eating something that appeared to be brown mush.

There was a blast of cold air behind them, and Lily and Buzz were pushed roughly into an open cage. Lily turned around to see a witch with a tarantula hat perched on her head.

"Good choice coming here," the witch sneered with a wicked smile on her face.

If I ever get home, no one is going to believe this, Lily thought.

"Who – or what – are you?" asked a soft voice.

They both turned to see a young lady, also a prisoner in one of the cages. She looked enchanted, because her skin was glowing.

"What does it *look* like we are," Buzz grumbled.

"Are you ... aliens?" the young lady asked.

"No, we are from a planet called Earth." Lily said.

"Oh. Well, I am the Queen of this land," the glowing lady whispered.

"Oh, and I am the queen of *our* land" Buzz mocked in a high-pitched voice.

"Sorry, he is just in a bad mood." Lily apologized to the Queen. "What's your name?"

"It's Abigail."

"My name's Lily, and he's Buzz" Lily declared, pointing to Buzz.

Suddenly there was a soft *bang*. Lily squinted into the darkness and saw the shadows approaching of two people and ... a baby elephant? A familiar face emerged from the darkness.

"Daniel!" Lily exclaimed, "Who are those, uh, people with you?"

"Long story. Just know that that's Pinky and that's Maridia," Daniel summed up. "Does anyone have a hairpin?"

"Doesn't that only work in the movie –" Buzz began.

CLICK

CLICK

CLICK

Daniel smoothly unlocked every door in the row.

"This really *should* be a movie," Buzz grumbled.

"You guys go! I'll come after I've unlocked every cage door and freed all these prisoners!"

Daniel, Lily, Buzz and the Sqoonafant

They hurried out of the dungeon and were about to step through the portal, but Pinky stopped them, motioning toward a display case, a glass globe sitting on a rose-colored marble pedestal.

"Is that the gem?" Pinky the Sqoonafant asked. Pinky moved closer to the pink, sparkling, jeweled heart and removed the glass covering it.

"ALERT! ALERT! ALERT!" the monitor exclaimed robotically.

"STOP RIGHT THERE!" yelled a loud, shrill voice.

Pinky grabbed the gem and made a run for it. All four of them jumped through the portal followed by all of the now-freed fairies. They could still hear the witch shouting "STOP THEM! STOP THEM!"

As they emerged from the portal, a stone wall slammed down from the ceiling, blocking their only way out.

"Everyone clasp hands!" Pinky shouted. He made a loud bellowing sound with his trunk. "I can transport us back to our city!"

"What? You can do *what*? Buzz asked. "This gets weirder every second!"

"Yes," Pinky said, and explained: "With a flash of her wand, one of the witches made me into ..." he glanced down at his Sqoonafant's body. "Well, *this*. I mean, I used to be a normal person. The only silver lining is the witch's wand also transferred a bit of its power to me. So, I can do a few cool things, like making us all disappear. Grab hands!"

CRACK!

Just like that they were back at the center of the city on the platform.

"Wow!" Lily exclaimed.

Pinky just smiled, and then raced over to the heart-shaped gem and replaced one of the half-hearts with the authentic one he had wrapped up in his trunk.

Nothing happened.

Realizing now which one was the fake, he reached to switch the real gem with the other half-heart but it was too late.

A screech filled the platform.

"STOPPPPPPPP!" yelled a witch.

Her skin was garbage-green and she was wearing the large tarantula hat. The witch flicked her arm toward them.

Daniel tried to move but couldn't. The green witch flicked her hand again, and Daniel and the others were forced to sit down. He moved the only part of him that remained unfrozen – his eyeballs – to look at Pinky, who was still standing.

"Oh – it's *you*," the witch looked at Pinky. "I remember you," she cackled.

She flicked her hand at Pinky. Everybody was watching Pinky in astonishment. His trunk was turning into a nose. His huge blue eyes were circling smaller into human-sized orbs. He grew handsomer by the minute! Daniel heard several gasps from behind him.

"I wish to duel against you once more," growled the witch. "I remember the day I met you. You pulled your sword on me, and we fought until your sword fell and I took it for my own." The witch pulled out a sword – his sword.

She continued, "I kept you imprisoned for one month. I took the DNA of what aliens call elephants and mixed it with the DNA of several other creatures and swirled it all into you, cursing you, making you into what you are. And soon after I cursed you, I examined the sword. I found the tiny opening in the bottom of the handle, the secret compartment – and the blue potion hidden inside. Three cups' worth. I tested some on my hawk and he began to grow clear and then vanished altogether. It was an invisibility potion! I poured it on myself and went to get the jeweled heart." That is how all of this happened. She dropped one heavy eyelid in a hideous wink.

She threw the prince his sword and drew out her wand. "I want to duel," she said again, a wicked smile twisting her features into something terrible. "On the count of three: 1 … 2 … FREEZE-elio" the witch pointed her wand at the prince. He dodged the curse easily.

"Hey! You didn't count to three," he yelled.

"I'm not supposed to tell the truth," she said, the same crooked smile revealing her mouthful of jagged, rotting teeth.

"Transform-elio! Dart Gun!" he yelled.

The sword immediately became smaller and then morphed into a tranquilizer dart gun.

BAM! He pressed the tiniest button on the side.

"REFLECT-elio!" the witch bellowed.

A purple bubble formed around the witch and the dart ricocheted harmlessly away.

Daniel watched in astonishment.

"COME-elio!" the witch said with a flick of her wand. Suddenly they heard a whooshing sound. A black broom came flying toward her and she hopped up on it. The broom flew swiftly up until she was out of sight. Suddenly they heard a piercing yell.

"FREEZE-elio," she shouted, flashing her wand toward the prince.

He dodged the shot but it hit a fairy that was watching the battle. The fairy's eyes opened wide, and she wasn't able to move. "Light-field-*elio*!" the prince shouted pointing his weapon.

A cone of purple light erupted from the barrel, a special light, a *magical* light, and when it covered the witch, who was trying to run away, it held her fast, the way a spider's web holds a fly.

Daniel watched as the witch performed a series of spells, trying to break free from the purple light, but none succeeded; the witch was trapped.

Suddenly Daniel was able to move again. He looked around and all the other creatures were starting to stand up as well.

"ILLUMIN-elio!" the Queen cried. A cage appeared around the witch. The cage was metal on the top and bottom, and the bars were red laser beams. The witch was not going anywhere.

"Everyone hurry back to the castle. Ali, Kate, you bring the cage to the castle!" the Queen – Abigail – said. Two beautiful fairies flew to the cage and lifted it easily off the ground, flying it toward the castle.

The Next Day

"Since we are back at the castle, I want to give very special thanks to someone," the Queen announced. "Daniel!"

Daniel began walking up the stage and as he did he looked down at Lily and Buzz's smiling faces. As soon as they had returned to the castle, Queen

Abigail had organized this beautiful ceremony. Fairies had dressed Daniel up in formal clothes just for the event.

The queen started her speech. "Since we know that this very special person – Daniel – has saved our lives, I would like to thank him with a little gift!"

Two small fairies flew over, carrying a wooden box. They set it on the floor. The queen opened it and with a playful smile hid the object it contained behind her back.

"Kneel down," she said.

Daniel did as he was told and then looked up at the queen. In her hand she held a sword. The handle was studded in sparkling gems

"For all the good deeds you have done, I now knight you," she said as she lowered the sword down to his shoulders, tapping first the left and then the right.

Daniel smiled, and then his face twisted into a question mark. "What about the Sqoona – er – Prince?" he asked.

"The prince is my son, named Prince Charming the Fourth. When he turned into a 'Squoonafant,' his brothers went looking for him but never found him. But *you* did – you found him and returned him to us." she answered. "He's in his room resting. And Daniel, for that you get more than just a knighting ceremony. You get one wish from me!"

Daniel looked at his friends as he thought of what wish he should choose. Then his eyes shined as he made his decision. "I know what I wish for," he announced, and grinned.

Epilogue: 1 Week Later

Finally, they were home! After the ceremony, the queen had indeed created a brand-new spaceship, which had been Daniel's wish; they had climbed on and flown back to Earth. As soon as they landed, the mission control team had rushed to them and begun asking questions, as if they were the new Neil Armstrong.

"Where were you?" one of them inquired.

"What happened?" another wanted to know.

Daniel looked at Lily and Buzz, all of them smiling at each other, and he said, "Well, that's a long story ..."

With Appreciation

Many people guided me in the right direction while I was writing this book. Without them, this book wouldn't exist. First, I would like to thank my mom who has encouraged me all the way. Next, I would like to thank Mr. Mark Price, my writing teacher, who was always encouraging and helpful while editing and working on my story. I would also like to thank Tatiana Minina for the beautiful front cover artwork she created for my book, and Lindsey Bainbridge, for her awesome job editing my manuscript.

Made in the USA
Columbia, SC
11 December 2018